caroline's cavy Goes camping

Other fiction titles by Melissa J. Taylor

Caroline's Cavy Series

Gram, Gramps, and a Guinea Pig Named Rover

The Guinea Pigs' Summer Storybook
The Guinea Pigs' Fall Storybook
The Guinea Pigs' Winter Storybook
The Guinea Pigs' Spring Storybook

caroline's cavy Goes camping

by Melissa J. Taylor

Caroline's Cavy Goes Camping
Copyright © 2013 by Melissa J. Taylor

Cover design and interior illustrations by Melissa J. Taylor

First printing 2013.

Summary: Caroline, her parents, and neighbor go on a camping trip with her young pet guinea pig in tow.

ISBN-13: 978-1490929354
ISBN-10: 1490929355

<u>Friday</u>

I sure enjoyed the pet show yesterday! Navy didn't win much of anything, but we got outside on a nice, sunshiny, happy day!

Today, getting the mail was the most exciting thing that happened.

If the flag is up, the mail hasn't come yet. Boo-hoo!

Sometimes summer days are like that and not much happens. I know grownups don't like it, but I like junk mail. You never know what you'll get free inside. It's like opening your stocking on Christmas morning. Sometimes there are coins, bookmarks, pads of paper, or stickers! The thickest junk mail is the best, because it can be packed. Sometimes there's more than one thing in an envelope.

Today junk mail came with a survey written on a postcard. Those types of things may look boring, but they can be as fun as anything else, as long as you know what to do with them. I filled it out, but I would never dare to send one in.

Please fill out this postpaid survey today to find out more about our revolutionary new weight loss product!

Your full name: Navy Blue.

Do you frequently have a full feeling?
Never! I could eat all day and never feel full.

Do you watch what you eat closely?
Yes, but that's tough to do when your eyes are on the sides of your head.

Have you spoken to your doctor about these distressing food-related issues?
I have tried, but my vet and I don't speak the same language!

Are you able to button your pants, even after a full meal?

I don't know. I don't wear them.

Please answer the following question to help us learn more about your eating style. If you could pick any one healthy food item from the following list to eat, which would it be? Apple, banana, beet, carrot, cereal, lettuce, parsley, salad greens.
Yes!

Would you like to learn more about our revolutionary new weight loss product that will help you lose at least five pounds per month?
No! If I lost five pounds, I would disappear!

After filling out the postcard, I set it up by Navy's cage in the kitchen, to be funny. That way, anyone who walks by her cage can read it.

Another ad that came in the mail today was for a full-color cooking magazine. It said it comes out every month and contains lots of recipes for different ways to cook vegetables. I didn't show that one to Navy. She might have really bought a subscription.

Saturday

I want to help my best friend get a guinea pig of her own. Not that Millie has ever said she wants one, or that I've ever told her my plan! But I'm sure she does want one. Who wouldn't? It's hard to get guinea pigs here. They must be popular. Mom had to reserve Navy, and most of the other guinea pigs at the pet store were reserved, too.

Both Millie and her little sister have friends with guinea pigs. I'm one of them. The friend, not the guinea pig. Guinea pigs are irresistible! Who wouldn't want one? And if Millie has a guinea pig, she and I can get together and have play dates with our guinea pigs. I picked up that term from adults. It's what they say when their children get together. Sometimes I think adults like to have terms for everything. I just call it something like, coming over. You don't have to schedule "coming over," and if you use the term "play date," it sounds like something you have to schedule. Kids aren't that way. We don't need to schedule having fun!

My mind turned to other things in the morning. Mom surprised me with something maybe even a little better to think about. At least for now. Because getting Millie a guinea pig is really exciting, but it can wait.

Mom woke me up this morning saying, "Caroline! On Friday, we're leaving to go camping for a week."

I jumped out of bed. "Hooray!" I love camping. There's nothing like it. You get away from everything in your house and get to be out in nature. A lot of kids might miss the television and things like that, but not me. I can do things like read a book, draw, or do a craft. Plus, you get to do all sorts of fun stuff like canoeing and foosball, or whatever activities the campground has.

CAMPING?!
"Water" we waiting for?
Ha ha.

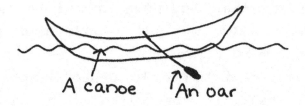

A canoe   An oar

Just as I was getting excited, though, Mom said, "I asked Millie's mom, and she can keep Navy at their house for the week we're gone."

My heart sank.

Me with a sunken heart.

I just got Navy! There's no way I can leave Navy all alone with a babysitter, even if Millie IS my very best friend and lives just across the street.

So, now I have a new plan. Navy needs to show Mom and Dad that she won't be any trouble and that she can go on the camping trip with us. I'm not really sure yet how to show them that. She's already just about as good as any guinea pig can be.

I wonder if they make sleeping bags in guinea pig sizes?

Navy in a
sleeping bag

Or air mattresses, so she could be extra nice and comfy? That probably wouldn't work. I'm lucky so far. Navy doesn't chew on things much. I have read that some guinea pigs are real chewers, because guinea pigs' teeth always grow and they have to keep chewing things to wear them down. Maybe it's because I'm a good guinea pig mom and give her wood to chew on.

The thing is, maybe I would like for her to be a chewer once school starts up again. I'm pretty good at getting homework done right away, but it sounds like a funny excuse. "But, Teacher, my guinea pig ate my homework!"

Even if she doesn't chew too much, I'd still worry about her having an air mattress. I don't use one, myself.

Air mattress + Navy
= BAD IDEA

POP!

Guinea pigs are almost magical animals. They can get all small and look round and short...

Same guinea pig.. two looks!

...and they can stretch and get really long and skinny. So even if they made sleeping bags and air mattresses for guinea pigs, I would never know what size to get for her, anyway.

I wish I could stretch and shrink like

a guinea pig. I could reach way up to get something off a high shelf, like, maybe a cookie jar that Mom had hidden out of reach, and then I could shrink way back down to normal so no one would suspect me.

It would be really neat if they made camping tents in guinea pig sizes. There would be mini zippers and teeny tiny doors, and little bitty windows that could be zipped open and closed.

But, if they really had this type of little guinea pig tent, Navy would maybe just go off on a camping trip all by herself.

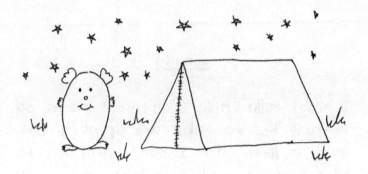

Sunday

I trust Millie. Millie is my best friend, so I trust her to take care of Navy. But, Navy is little, and I don't want her to forget me. A week is a long time for a little baby guinea pig to be away from someone she's supposed to be getting to know. What if I get back from camping, only to find out that Millie and Navy are best friends? I would lose both of my best friends, just like that!

This afternoon, I found Mom sitting in the living room. I sat down on the couch across from her and placed Navy on my lap. "Mom, I want to take Navy on the trip." I looked down at Navy. "How can you say 'no' to her?"

She shook her head. "Caroline, I don't think it would be kind to Navy to take her with us."

I frowned and scratched Navy under her chin. "But Stanley's family takes Taco on trips!"

Mom smiled at me. "Caroline, that's true. But dogs like to be with people. A dog is at home anywhere his people are. Guinea pigs like their homes, and Navy is just barely getting used to her cage. She might feel nervous being away from it."

That made me feel sad. I think Navy likes me, not just her cage. She's really starting to purr when I pet her. "She wouldn't be at our home if she's with Millie here OR with me camping. At least with me, she would be with family. I could keep her in her little pen, which she likes just as much as her cage."

Mom still said no. "She jumps out of that pen, so even if she did go, she could only be in that pen in the tent. Outside, she would have to be in her pet carrier. That doesn't seem nice, now, does it?"

I jutted out my lower lip to pout. "Can you resist this face?" I asked Mom as best I could. (It's pretty hard to talk when you're wearing that kind of face.)

She laughed. "Yes, yes I can."

I wrinkled my nose. "Oh, rats!"

I put Navy back in her cage in the kitchen. I walked over to the fridge to get a drink of water from a pitcher in the fridge. That's when it happened. I accidentally brushed against a plastic bag on the fridge shelf.

From her cage, Navy called out. "Wheeek! Wheeek!"

Mom ran to the kitchen as fast as she could. "Oh, that's so cute!"

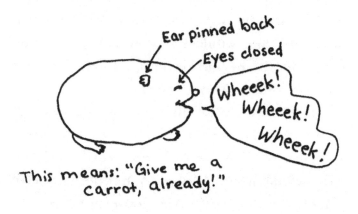

Ear pinned back

Eyes closed

Wheeek! Wheeek! Wheeek!

This means: "Give me a carrot, already!"

It's hard to believe such a tiny little animal can make such a big noise. She pinned her teensy ears back and opened her mouth and squealed like a siren. We gave her a bit of carrot to reward her for finally learning how to ask us for food.

I have to say, she asks for food just about as politely as my neighbor Stanley.

Monday

Millie came over today. The very first thing she said was, "Do you want to play with Navy?"

We went into the kitchen and got Navy out of her cage. She's a lot friendlier than she used to be. We put her on the kitchen floor and put our feet touching each other's to make a little place for her to play.

Millie smiled over at me. "I'm excited about getting to watch Navy."

That reminded me that Navy would be with her for a whole week, and made me feel worried. Millie didn't know that I don't want her babysitting Navy for a whole week. "I want her to be with me. I've simply begged about it."

Millie frowned. "I've never had a pet before, Caroline, but I promise I'll take really good care of her." She looked hurt, and that made me feel really bad.

"Millie, it's not that I don't trust you. You're really good at playing with Navy. It's only that I just got her. I don't want to be away from her for a whole week. She might forget me!"

"You know, I have your school photo framed and in my room," Millie said. She patted Navy on the head when Navy ran over to her. "I can show her your picture every day. I won't let her forget you."

It didn't seem the same to me. Then I realized why. "I think it's not just that I don't want her to forget me. It's also that I will miss her."

Millie nodded. "I understand. But you know how to draw. You can take your journal with you and draw about her any time you think about her."

That's why Millie is such a good friend. She's understanding, and she knows just how I feel. That's also why she deserves a guinea pig of her own some day.

After we played with Navy, I got out some embroidery thread. A lot of people call it embroidery floss, but that makes me think of something I have to do to my teeth and am not always so good at remembering.

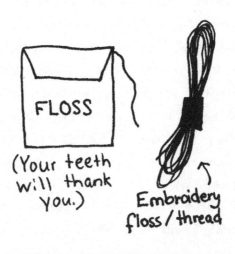

FLOSS

(Your teeth will thank you.)

Embroidery floss/thread

"What are you going to do with that?" Millie asked.

"I want to do a wrap in your hair." I just started doing this, and practiced by taping threads of embroidery floss to my nightstand and wrapping more floss around it. You take the thread and you wrap it around and around until you're at the very end of the hair. You can also put in knots, and they will spiral down the length of the wrap. It can be all sorts of colors.

Millie has short hair, so she was the perfect person to put my first hair wrap on. I braided a small section of her hair, and then started at the top and worked my way down. She wanted colors like purple, blue, and light green, even though they didn't match her red striped T-shirt.

She may have short hair, but it still took a long time and a lot of work. I couldn't really take breaks because I worried it would come undone and I'd have to start all over again.

When I finished, it looked even better than I thought it would. We went to the big bathroom mirror so Millie could admire it.

Millie, with a beautiful hair wrap. (It took a whole hour!)

"Why don't you put one of these in your hair?" Millie asked, as she picked up the hair wrap and tried to look at the end of it.

She touched on a sore spot with me. I have curly hair. If I put a wrap in my hair, it would get swallowed up by the waves. Sometimes, I want straight hair more than anything. But Mom told me if I had straight hair, the thing I would want most in the world would be for my hair to be curly. "It wouldn't work on me."

"Well," said Millie, "you can practice as much as you want on me. Maybe my whole hair could be full of them. It's the best hair accessory ever!"

A little bit after Millie went home, the phone rang.

"Caroline," Mom called me, "it's Millie's mom. She wants to know, 'How do I get this thing out of my daughter's hair?'"

Oops.

Tuesday

It's late at night, so I'm writing this with a flashlight under the covers.

I have some not-so-good news and some hopefully good news I just had to write down. It's that type of really big news that simply can't wait until tomorrow.

When I said goodnight to Mom tonight and got tucked in, she told me some big news in a quick way that meant she didn't want it to sound like big news. "By the way, Stanley is coming with us."

"Stannie the Meanie! He CAN'T!" I kind

of yelled the last part. "NOOO!"

I puffed out my cheeks and lower lip to give Mom my best, extra-big, pouty face. I sometimes call my neighbor Stannie the Meanie. Mom watches him a lot when his mom is out. Their family has a little dog. The one they take on trips.

Stanley ↑   Taco ↖
            the dog

"He can," she said. "And don't let me

catch you calling him names. His parents are going to be especially busy this coming week at their store. They have an employee going away on vacation, and his mom needs to fill in that person's hours."

Stanley's dad owns the grocery store, and a lot of times Stanley's mom has to help him out there. Mom watches Stanley a lot when his mom is doing that or running other errands.

Mom kept talking. "His mom was going to need me to watch him quite a bit, but we won't be here. I told her, we would be happy to have Stanley come along!"

"WE would be happy? Nobody asked me." Sometimes when I get bad news, I find it really hard to sleep. Good news, too. Either kind makes me think so much, I can't have an empty, quiet mind that feels like resting. I knew I wouldn't be getting much sleep tonight. "Maybe someone else can watch him, so we can have a Stanley break."

"Caroline, life is all about there being a balance between good things and bad things." Mom smiled down at me and patted me on the head. "Besides, you'll have someone there near your age to do things with. That should be fun! Maybe you'll realize Stanley isn't so bad, huh?"

I didn't think so. Then, I had an idea. "If Stanley is going, I should be allowed to take Navy."

Mom stopped for a minute. That was good. Sometimes when you ask something, parents will just say "no" right away, without thinking about it. If they think about something for a bit, it can sometimes end up being good news.

"All right, Caroline. If the weather looks like it's going to have comfortable temperatures for her, then she can come along."

I threw off the covers and got out of bed to give her a big hug. "Oh, thank you, thank you!"

"And we have to see if the campground allows pets. I'll call them tomorrow."

So, that's the good news. I am hoping it's good news, anyway. It's hard to wait until tomorrow to find out if they allow pets. I'm going to turn my flashlight off now and try to get to sleep. That's asking a lot!

Wednesday

Today, Mom called the campground. I begged and begged her to let me listen in on the other phone, and she let me. "Just don't scream if they say pets are allowed."

I agreed, although I knew it would be really tough to hold in my excitement. I can get really excited sometimes. I promised myself I would just jump if they said it was okay to take Navy.

She called on the phone in the kitchen, and I went to pick up the receiver in the family room.

I held my breath as she asked. "Hi! My daughter and I are calling to find out if pets are allowed on the campground. She has a little guinea pig she would like to bring along."

I couldn't hold my breath any longer, so I put my hand over the receiver so they couldn't hear me.

"That should be fine," the other person's voice said. "We allow small dogs and other animals, as long as they aren't loose."

I did it--I jumped up right then and there. I only yelled in my head.

—Hooray!——

This afternoon, Mom surprised me with some more news. "Caroline, we need to practice clipping Navy's toenails."

Guinea pigs have nails that never stop growing. If the nails aren't clipped, they can grow too long and hurt your guinea pig's toes.

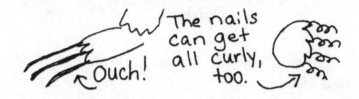

Ouch!

The nails can get all curly, too.

I have no idea why guinea pigs are made this way. How do they clip their nails in the wild? Do they chew them all off?

Munch munch crunch

Navy's nails weren't super long yet, but, because they had never been clipped in her whole life, they were sharp and felt like little pins poking into my skin.

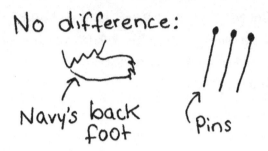

No difference:

Navy's back foot

Pins

Mom gathered a towel, flashlight, and nail clippers.

Towel + Flashlight + Nail clippers

= Watch out, Navy!!!

I got Navy from the kitchen, and we all sat down on the living room couch.

Mom held up each item as she spoke. "The towel is to wrap Navy in, so she's not as squirmy, and to keep her comfortable."

"You hear that, Navy?" I said. "It won't be such a big deal, and you'll be all cozy in the towel."

Mom held up the clippers. "The nail clippers are toenail clippers."

I was really surprised at how scary they looked, when compared to Navy's small size. "Mom, they're so big. Can't we use fingernail ones?"

She shook her head. "Fingernail clippers have more of a curve to them. We need to be very careful to hold these sideways from the way her nails grow, and to make a straight cut. If these intimidate you, then you could get some special pet clippers from the store."

"Intimidate" means that they make you nervous. I shook my head. "We can try it. What's the flashlight for?"

Mom turned it on, and then back off again. "Guinea pigs have a 'quick.' If you cut down too low, blood will come out from the toenail. We don't want to hurt Navy, so we'll hold the flashlight up to her nails to help avoid the quick."

"That's a lot of work!" I said. "I'm glad I don't have to hold a flashlight when I clip MY nails."

"It's because she's a red guinea pig. If she were a different color, she might have light toenails."

We started with Navy's back right foot. I held the flashlight and Navy, and watched as Mom carefully lined up the clippers. "Don't clip until you are positive that you are clipping only nail and that Navy isn't going to squirm," Mom said. She clipped.

Navy screamed at the top of her lungs.

"Mom! Mom! You got her quick!" I felt like I was going to cry.

"I did no such thing," Mom said. She clipped one more nail. Navy screamed again. "I think we'll stop for today. We can do a bit each day, but I don't want to stress her out."

Twelve more nails to go! I sure am glad guinea pigs don't have twenty nails to clip like we do. I think Navy would rather have long nails like the kind you would see in a horror movie, instead of getting them clipped.

She's too cute to be scary!

I know someone who says he clips his toenails by sticking his foot in his mouth. That's disgusting. I won't say who it is, but he does live next door to me.

Thursday

Because Stanley and Navy are going to be in the great outdoors together, I have A PLAN. Stanley doesn't like her. He calls her a furry potato. Not to get too technical or anything, but guinea pigs don't even have fur. They have hair. But try telling Stanley anything.

I bet I call it fur sometimes, too, so I won't even try.

To be honest, he's never really met Navy enough to know whether or not he likes her. Her cage is in the kitchen, so he passes her, but there hasn't ever been a formal introduction. "Navy, meet Stanley. Stanley, meet Navy. Now, shake hands. Or, paws. Or hand and paw, I guess."

Maybe I need to make sure the camping trip becomes Project Stanley and Navy Become Best Friends. No, I don't like that. I'm her best friend. Maybe Operation Stanley and Navy Become Second Best Friends. Oh, but that leaves out Millie, Dad, and Mom. Okay, maybe just Project Stanley and Navy Decide to Be on Speaking Terms.

Even THAT would be an improvement.

I packed today. That's something a lot of kids my age might have their parents do for them. Not me.

Some suitcase essentials:

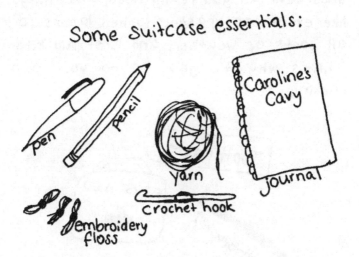

pen
pencil
yarn
Caroline's Cavy journal
crochet hook
embroidery floss

I wanted to have lots of space in my

suitcase for things like my journal, books, pens, pencils, markers, embroidery thread, yarn to crochet with, a ball, a small blanket to hold Navy in, and other things that have to come first before clothes. One of the things I had to pack was vitamin C, since guinea pigs don't make their own. (I guess they don't know the recipe.) You have to be sure your pet guinea pig gets vitamin C, or she can get really sick.

Parents would make sure you reserved room in your suitcase for twice as much underwear as you really need, and things like extra toothpaste, clothes layers for all sorts of weather, and First Aid kits. That's why it's good to do your own packing.

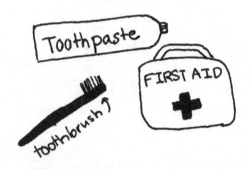

I had to sit on the suitcase and hop my "backside" up and down on it in order to smash the top down far enough to latch it shut.

Even though I packed my journal, I realized later--when I sat down and wanted to write in it--that you can't exactly USE your journal when it's locked away in a suitcase. Oops. I'll just have to remember to pack this before we leave.

Mom and I finished up clipping the rest of Navy's nails today. We wanted to make sure we were all done before leaving, so she could feel like she was getting a vacation, too. We did just a bit at a time and gave her lots of breathers, carroty rewards, and praise. I even clipped two nails all on my own!

 Showing off her sparkly manicure.

She got a beautiful new manicure just in time for her camping trip.

That sounds a little backwards!

Friday

Stanley's mom had to leave before we did, so he came over a bit before we left to go camping. Mom asked him a lot of questions that showed she was born to be a mom.

Suitcase   Sleeping bag

"Did you pack your toothbrush?"

"Yes."

"Did you pack a swimsuit?"

"Yes."

"Did you recall that you would need a sleeping bag?"

He pointed at it.

"Did you bring a jacket? Nights can get cold."

He nodded.

"Did you pack extra shoes?"

"Yes."

"Did you pack fourteen pairs of underwear?"

(See what I mean?)

After that, Stanley and I went to sit out on the back patio while Mom and Dad packed up the car with our tent, all of Mom's kitchen-away-from-home things, and our other camping gear.

"You'll like camping," I said.

He picked at a scab on his knee. He seems to always have a lot of them. Scabs. He only has TWO knees.

"I don't know," he said. "Never been."

Stanley, picking at a scab.

Me, trying not to notice.

"I've never been to this campground," I said. "Mom and Dad picked it out because it has a rec center with lots of activities, and swimming and boating, and lots of trees. It sounds really pretty, but it's kind of far away. But the best thing of all is that I get to take Navy!"

He scowled. "I should be allowed to take Taco, then!"

I hadn't thought of that! "Taco might scare Navy. Besides, your parents will be with him."

After some last-minute "pit stops" and lots of double-checking to make sure the main camp supplies were packed, we were off to go camping. It couldn't have come soon enough. When you're really excited about something, every minute seems to last for an hour.

I didn't like having a long car trip there. We had never been to this camping place before. It's farther away than other ones we've gone to, but Mom and Dad thought it sounded like it had a lot of things to do at it, so they wanted to try something different.

After we picked out a campsite, we

got out of the car and stretched our legs.

Navy, in her carrier, grumbled in the way that means she doesn't like something, but I promised her there aren't any scary things like bears here. If there ARE any bears here, I'm sure they would find other things to eat than guinea pigs, like marshmallows and hot dogs and campfire pies.

Oh! I'll make some s'mores!

marshmallows

I breathed in all the wonderful fresh air.

Stanley said, "This place smells like a car air freshener." You can tell when someone has never been camping before.

It smells like pine, a lovely sweet and sharp and tangy smell. The ground is a mix of dirt and dried pine needles that make crunching sounds when I walk on them.

What stanley smells   What I smell

We have a big green and white tent. I think it could hold maybe eight people if they were lined up like sardines. It will be good to have some wiggle room since there are five of us.

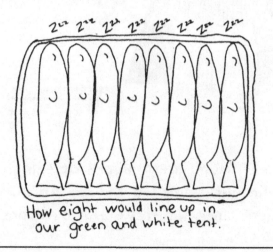

How eight would line up in our green and white tent.

Mom and Dad set up the tent together.

When we go camping, Mom likes to have the outdoors set up almost like it's indoors. It's like a home-away-from-home that's outside.

I put Navy's carrier on the picnic table to watch while Mom and Dad hung a rope up between two trees. It's for putting up things like wet towels or swimsuits to dry.

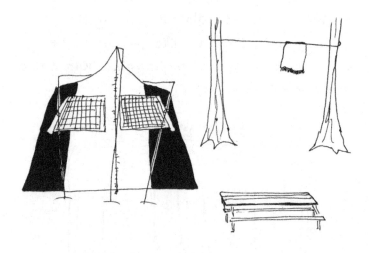

Next, Mom got a bunch of things out of the car trunk to set up an outdoor kitchen. Since we treat the outdoors like it's indoors, we make billions of mosquitoes really happy when we camp.

Mom stayed with Navy at our campsite after things were set up, so the rest of us could look around. While we were leaving, she held up a plastic bag. "Look! I packed carrots!" Moms think of everything.

It felt magical to walk into the rec center. It had a really musty smell like moss and mildew and old wood. All sorts of entertaining things were crammed inside the building, like pinball, arcade games, table tennis, shuffleboard, and even a jukebox. An older boy with brown hair was putting sand on the shuffleboard table. That might sound kind of silly, but it's normal.

"It smells like my grandma's basement in here!" Stanley complained.

Seriously, Stanley needs to get out more.

Saturday

I held Navy last night for a while, after we all got into our sleeping bags.

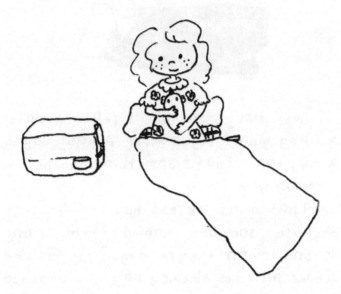

I said, "Stanley, I hope you and Navy decide to like each other."

Stanley placed his flashlight up to his face, and I could see him scowling. "All she does is sit and do nothing. What good is a guinea pig? If Taco were here, we'd be doing all sorts of stuff together. Dogs are better than guinea pigs."

"Well, Navy is a PUP." I felt desperate. A baby guinea pig is a pup. A baby dog is a pup, too. "That's something she has in common with Taco."

That didn't impress him at all. "Just because someone named them wrong doesn't mean they're dogs." He crawled deeper into his sleeping bag and switched his flashlight off.

I put Navy in her small pen so she could go to sleep.

I have the best sleeping bag in the

world. I don't know why, but it just reminds me of camping. I bet a lot of girls my age would want one that's pink and has flowers all over it, or something like that. Or maybe puppies or kittens. Not real puppies or kittens, but drawings of them.

Mine isn't like that at all. It's dark red, and the inside is soft flannel in a red and green plaid pattern. It reminds me of Christmas. That has nothing to do with summer or camping, but Christmas makes me feel all warm and fuzzy, and so does camping. Somehow, that just makes it seem like the perfect sleeping bag! BUT, flannel can be a little hot in the summer sometimes, unless it gets nice and cool outside. The best camping weather is a little bit hot during the day, but really nice and cool at night.

Camping is kind of noisy, especially if there are crickets and little tree frogs around your tent,

creak
creak
creak

Or there are sometimes large snaps and cracks from things falling out of trees. Some people who want to scare you will tell you those snaps and cracks are Bigfoot or the bogeyman, but we campers know better. There's nothing really too scary about those noises-- unless a limb falls on your tent!

Bigfoot ↗

Tent walls are very thin. It's like sleeping with paper all around you, it's that thin. It's even harder to sleep if someone you know happens to snore.

I am not sure if I should have put that down on paper, because it might embarrass someone named Stanley.

When I woke up this morning, Mom told me that I looked a mess, the way only a mom could, because if a friend told you, you'd just be mad. I remembered to pack a lot of fun things, but I forgot to pack my comb. My hair is curly, so it's not the kind of hair you want to comb. But if you don't comb it at all, then it might turn into an even BIGGER tangled mess. There's no way to win with this hair. I think my hair may even have leaves and pine needles stuck in it.

What's hiding in my hair?

caterpillar

pine needles

leaves

Mom said if I'm not careful, some birds will come along and build a nest in it. I think that might be kind of fun.

Doing my part to help
the environment.

Today, I went swimming in the pond here. I didn't mean to go swimming, but I'll get to that! The pond isn't big, but it has fish in it that tickled my toes. This is something that Navy couldn't share with me. I know her big cousin is called a capybara. They're HUGE rodents that look like giant guinea pigs. They have webbed toes, and they like to swim! If I could, I would have a pet capybara. Mom and Dad told me one would eat so many greens, our lawn would just up and disappear. It would save Dad some trouble with mowing, I figure. But I suppose I'll never get one.

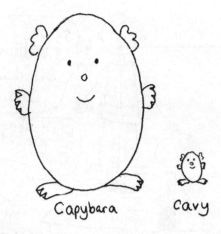

Capybara   Cavy

Dad, Stanley, and I put on puffy orange lifejackets and went canoeing. We tried to, anyway. I think we should have used the paddleboats, since they have big bottoms (kind of like Navy!). They're a lot more stable than a tipsy canoe.

You shouldn't let someone who has never been in a canoe before get in a canoe right after you do. That person may not know how to get in a wobbly boat. I got in the canoe first, and while Dad stood on the dock waiting for his turn, Stanley got in. He stood too far to one side and tipped it right over. SPLASH!

We both went into the water.

"Do you feel any fish in there?" Dad asked, safe and dry on the dock.

I felt them nibbling my toes as I treaded water. "Yes. Hungry ones, too!"

His eyes got really big, and so did his smile. As soon as he pulled us out and we got back to our campsite, he and Stanley walked off with fishing gear. Stanley didn't even bother to dry off. He kept on all of his wet clothes, including his shoes and socks. They made squishing sounds as he walked away.

I changed and hung my wet clothes up on the rope Mom and Dad had put between two trees.

I sure was glad Navy hadn't gone with me. She's not a webbed-footed capybara, and I don't think they make life jackets in her size.

Sunday

Last night we had a campfire, partly so I could put my clothes near it to help them dry out! Stanley was still soaked through.

Before starting the campfire, Dad made us some roasting sticks from fallen sticks he found in our campsite.

Mom washed them in her outdoor kitchen with some of the water she had brought along, all stored in plastic milk bottles. "We don't know where these sticks have been!"

Dad laughed. "In a tree!"

Mom used two fingers to "walk" along one of them. "Well, then, we don't know whose dirty little feet have walked all over them. Those birds and squirrels! Besides, you found these lying on the ground."

Dad laughed again. "Sometimes I wonder if you would wash a bar of soap!"

"Why?" Mom asked. "Do you have one that needs washing?"

After finishing the sticks, Dad made a campfire in the fire pit out of larger branches. We gathered around it, and he handed us each a stick.

The type of roasting stick Dad makes:

The kind I would rather have:

The air smelled all chilly and like pine and burning wood. I shuddered a little bit as Mom grabbed a bag of marshmallows and handed us each one to put on our stick. I don't know if I shuddered because of the cool breeze, or because there's just nothing that is much more exciting than sitting around a campfire and roasting marshmallows!

Dad and Mom sat on some green folding chairs.

Stanley and I dragged the picnic table over to sit on its bench backwards. I put Navy's carrier on top.

My favorite marshmallow color is an

in between color. It's almost pinkish orange, just barely heated up so that it's all ooey gooey but not burnt. Thankfully, there's usually someone in your family who likes dark brown or black marshmallows, so you can just pass along the mistakes.

The flames flickered, and we all looked a little creepy with our orange-glowing faces.

Dad said, "I'm going to tell a spooky story."

Mom gave him a look that said, "Oh no you don't." She shook her finger at him, too.

Dad started, anyway. Mom had nothing to be worried about, really. I saw Dad looking at Navy's carrier on the picnic table. Navy gave him the idea for his story. "Once upon a time, there was a guinea pig that had red glowing eyes and fangs."

Stanley interrupted. "You mean, the fangs were red and glowing?"

Dad looked a little shocked. "Uh, no. Only the eyes were red and glowing. Where was I? Oh, yeah, the guinea pig had red glowing eyes and fangs."

Stanley interrupted again. "You just said the fangs WEREN'T red and glowing. Besides, does this HAVE to be about guinea pigs?!"

Mom shook her head. "I think Stanley has had too much sugar."

Just then, Stanley pointed up in the sky. "LOOK! A big flock of birds!"

Late at night? I didn't have the heart to tell him they were bats.

This morning, I wanted more than anything to go to the rec center. Stanley wanted to, too, so we walked there together.

"What's that?" Stanley asked as we got close. There was a handwritten sign on the door.

I ran ahead and up the steps to the door and read the sign. It said "CLOSED." "Why would they close the rec center?" I looked at the sign closely, and my head felt all fuzzy. Not just because my hair was in a tangled mess, either. "It's supposed to be open every day, even weekends." Something didn't feel right.

Stanley kicked the wood steps leading into the building. He ran up the steps and reached in front of me to try the door. "It's locked."

Stanley and I walked back down the steps and to the campsite.

"Mom," I said, "why would the rec center be closed today?"

She looked up from working on lunch and shrugged her shoulders. "It's closed?"

Stanley and I nodded.

"I don't know. Maybe they had to do some maintenance today. That's odd for a Sunday, though, I would think."

Stanley and I went miniature golfing instead. The course that the camp has isn't as nice as the ones where you pay to play. Normal miniature golf courses have exciting obstacles like drawbridges and swinging wood poles and traps. This one is different. Hole one obstacle: a big rock. Hole two obstacle: a big rock. Hole three obstacle: a big rock. And so on, for each one.

GOLF HOLE OBSTACLES:

① A rock   ② A rock   ③ A rock

④ A rock   ⑤ A rock   ⑥ A rock

⑦ A rock   ⑧ A rock   ⑨ Guess.

It's kind of hard to get too excited about playing a game when every single obstacle is a rock right in front of a hole.

There are only nine holes in the camp's miniature golf course, instead of eighteen.

I guess they ran out of rocks.

Monday

This morning, I really wanted to go to the rec center. There are so many things to do! Dad had brought along a bunch of quarters, and he gave them to me in case Stanley and I wanted to play the arcade games or use the jukebox.

It will play anything you want. As long as the song is really, really old.

The rec center was empty, but open!

Stanley and I started playing table tennis. Stanley has better reflexes than I do. He could get the ball even when I thought it was going to hit the edge and earn me a point. Not on purpose, because I can't aim. Maybe he has quick reflexes from playing with his dog so much.

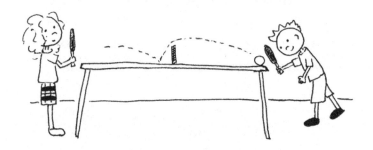

I finally started almost getting the hang of it when some older boys came in, one with brown hair and one with blonde. The one with darker hair had been using the shuffleboard on Friday.

They walked up to the table tennis and stood there staring at us.

"Hey! We're going to play that now," the kid with blonde hair said. I could tell

he meant business. He grabbed the ball
as it bounced to Stanley.

"We're using it," Stanley said.
"Caroline just got started being able to
play. Sort of."

I scrunched up my nose at him. Sure,
it's true. But THEY didn't need to know
that.

"We don't care. We're here to use it,
and that's that," the boy with brown
hair said. He lunged at Stanley's paddle
and grabbed it from him.

"You said it, Abe!" Then we knew the
brown haired boy's name was Abe.

Stanley has more bravery than brains sometimes. He walked around Abe, and grabbed the paddle back!

After that, Stanley started slapping at the kid with the paddle!

Lesson I learned:
Don't cross Stanley!

One thing bad about that rec center is that it's a closed-off building, and it doesn't have stuff most adults would like in it, like car magazines and makeup. We were the only ones in there, so no one could see that the big kids were picking on us little kids.

"Knock it off, kid!" Abe said. "Seth, get that paddle from that little girl. I can just use my hand."

The blonde boy grabbed at my paddle, but I didn't put up much of a fight. Well, really, I didn't put up ANY of a fight. I handed it to him as soon as Abe told him to take it. Stanley went right on hitting Abe with his paddle, though.

Abe pushed Stanley away with a shove, and served the ball with his hand. Seth used my paddle.

"Bullies!" Stanley yelled at them.

"Come on, Stanley," I said. "We can play the arcade games."

He tossed the paddle onto the floor and scowled at Abe's back.

We walked over to the arcade games, all lined up in a row.

Favorite food: quarters !

Stanley said he was going to get his initials on the high scores list, but the quarters got eaten really fast.

I guess Stanley is about as good at arcade games as I am at table tennis.

Tuesday

Dad and Stanley decided to play catch at the campsite. "If I had my DOG here, he would catch the ball," Stanley said to me. I knew he meant that was something better than Navy can do.

She can't catch a ball... but she's still cute!

Poor Navy! I think she must have her feelings hurt. Too bad she's not like the guinea pig in Dad's horror story. She could take a good bite out of Stanley, just like the mosquitoes are doing. I'm very fortunate. The mosquitoes like

Stanley more than they like me. I don't know why they do, but at least I've found a good reason to have him camping with us.

After they finished, I asked Stanley if he wanted to go to the rec center again. He looked down at the ground and shuffled his feet in the carpet of fallen pine needles.

I looked at him and wondered what was going on. Then I remembered Abe and Seth. "Oh, Dad. Do you think you could go there with us? Maybe you would like some of the stuff there."

He nodded. "Sure! I can go with you two."

We walked to the rec center.

Abe and Seth were there again. Two large foldout tables were set up in the middle of the room, and the table tennis was folded in half and sitting in a corner. They were playing with the arcade games. They looked at us and their eyebrows pointed down when they saw Dad. They slinked out of the rec center as if they knew they had done something wrong and were in trouble.

I wondered what the tables were set up for.

A lady walked up to us. "Hi! I'm Nora. We're having a lanyard making activity for kids later today. Every time I have put up signs about it in here, they've disappeared!" She looked at Stanley and me. "Would you like to come?" She held one up and showed us the lanyard. It looked like a necklace, only one half of cord continued down farther, with a whistle attached to the end of it. The lanyard had four sides to it, like a square.

Nora

lanyard

whistle

We both nodded. I liked the lanyard and the idea of doing a special camping craft. I figured Stanley liked the thought of having a whistle.

"Come back at two," she said. "We'll have it all set up by then, and you can meet some of the other kids staying at the campground."

If they were like the two we'd already met, I kind of hoped no one would show up.

We went back at two, and those older kids weren't there. There were a lot of other kids there, though. Stanley went off to sit at the boys' table, and I went to sit in a foldout chair at the girls' table, with my back to the boys.

I don't think that Nora meant for there to be a special boys' table and a special girls' table, but that probably shows she doesn't understand kids very well.

Nora showed us how to work with the plastic cord, called gimp.

"I will hand out the whistles when you're finished," Nora said.

I could tell she at least understood something about boys. Handing out the whistles first would only mean trouble.

The gimp was on big spools.

Making a lanyard is kind of like weaving, and once you get used to it, it's easy and fun. The colors I chose to work with were blue and green. You can talk while you're working on making a lanyard, because it doesn't really take a lot of brain power. The rec center got really loud.

"I'm Mia," the girl sitting next to me said, just after I'd gotten the hang of the craft. She worked with pink and purple gimp.

"I'm Caroline," I said.

Mia

"I haven't seen you in the rec center. Did you just come to the campground?"

"No." She shook her head. "My little sister and I have been here a whole week already. We just don't come in the rec center now that THEY'RE here."

"Never," a little girl sitting across from us said. She stuck out her tongue, then went back to staring at her gimp. I figured she was Mia's little sister.

I knew just who they meant. "You mean, those two older boys, Abe and Seth?"

"They act like they own the place," Mia said. "They even put a sign up that said the rec center is closed, so they could have it all to themselves!"

So that had been THEM! The rec center hadn't really been closed on Sunday.

"But, it's not so bad," she said. "There are other things to do around here, like taking out the paddleboats or canoeing. Anywhere adults are, they're not going to be around. When there are activities here, too, it's okay, because there are grownups."

I frowned. None of it seemed fair. No wonder the rec center looked so empty all the time.

Mia smiled. "Anyway, have you gone canoeing yet?"

"No, but we tried. I have before at other campgrounds. I'm not very good at paddling, though!"

Mia smiled. "The first time we went canoeing, our dad just kept the paddle on one side and made us go in a circle."

We laughed. You can't do that. You have to paddle on both sides, or you'll just go around and around and never get anywhere.

We kept talking about fun camping memories, until Nora said it was time to leave so that they could clean up the rec center and get it back to normal.

I looked around. I didn't see Stanley, but most projects I could see at the boys' table didn't look anything like the lanyard craft. They had made other things out of the gimp, like knots and tangles. One boy had wrapped a lot together and was trying to see if it would work like a baseball. "No way was I going to wear a necklace!" he said. He hadn't rolled it tightly, and the whole thing started falling apart when it hit a wall.

Nora handed out the whistles. No one had finished the craft. I guess she hadn't really thought about how long it would take to make something that big. Or that boys might not want to do it at all. "You can take extra gimp back to your campsite to finish the craft." She looked a little tired to me.

When Stanley and I left the rec

center, he kept blowing his whistle over and over again. I asked him what he had done with the gimp.

"Nothing," he said.
"Nothing?!"
"Nuh-uh. A kid named Max and I were by that one wall, playing shuffleboard."
How he still managed to get a whistle out of Nora is beyond me.

Wednesday

We forgot to ask Dad to go to the rec center with us this morning. Well, maybe we didn't really FORGET. After we all got back to our campsite from swimming together, Dad went fishing, and Mom left to play miniature golf. I told her not to be TOO disappointed. Stanley and I decided to sit in the tent and play cards.

"I have something I can do," I said. I grabbed my embroidery thread and asked him to sit in front of me. "It's a stylish hair thing."

Normally, I would never touch Stanley's hair. Normally, Stanley wouldn't let me, anyway. But you can only play Go Fish so many times before you start to go loopy.

I quickly noticed that his hair isn't long enough to do anything fun with it.

It's not even as long as Millie's hair. You can make a hair wrap longer by using embroidery thread as if it's hair and wrapping it. I kept going and going, because otherwise he wouldn't have had much of a wrap in his hair.

"What are you doing?" he asked. Stanley is not very patient.

"Something really neat!" I kept going and going.

Stanley kept complaining. I tell you, he is not very patient.

After over an hour, I decided it was long enough to finish off.

My longest hair wrap
EVER!

Stanley reached up to touch his hair, running his fingers along it, and I guess realizing part of his hair seemed a lot longer. "Hey!" He didn't sound very happy. Stanley jumped up and ran out of the tent. When he came back, he wore a scowl and flung the embroidery thread at me. I guess it comes out really easily if you have short, short hair. "I went to the men's bathroom to look in the mirror. When I saw it, I ripped it out. You made me look like a GIRL."

I'm starting to think the embroidery thread was a waste of my allowance.

Stanley shrugged off his anger, and got brave. "Let's go to the rec center and hope those kids aren't there."

"I can't leave Navy all alone."

"Take her, then," he said.

I agreed right away, because I thought she might like to see it.

I did something wrong. More than one thing wrong, because we should have never gone to the rec center without an adult. I made it even worse taking Navy, and not taking her the right way. I should have put her in her carrier. I know I should have. Being with Stanley, I wanted him to think of Navy in a different way. Dogs don't have to be in carriers, and he's used to being with Taco. Having Navy in a carrier somehow made her seem like less of a pet than a dog. So, I just carried her.

When we got there, I showed Navy around, but I couldn't do much since I had to hold her. I showed her the arcade games and the jukebox that will play any song you want it to, as long as it's a song that's so old that you've never even heard of it.

As I walked over to the shuffleboard, my eyes caught some movement outside. I looked out the window, and my heart sank. Abe and Seth were outside, and they were climbing up the stairs to the rec center!

"Quick!" I said to Stanley. I shoved Navy toward him. "Put Navy under your shirt! If you don't, they might hurt her!"

I would have done it, but we had been swimming early in the morning, and I only had a swimsuit and shorts on.

Stanley hid her under his shirt without complaining even once. I really had to hand it to him. Well, I handed Navy to him, too. But I mean he really stepped up and didn't let me down. He got her hidden just in time.

Stanley looked like he had eaten a bowling ball.

They came inside and walked up to us. They looked at Stanley, up and down. "What have you got in your shirt, huh?" Abe asked. "Are you hiding the table tennis paddle from me?"

Stanley looked brave. "You need to leave me alone! I have NAVY with me!"

That kid's eyes shot open so wide!

"What Navy?! The WHOLE Navy?"

Stanley looked at him and said each word carefully and slowly. "The. WHOLE. Navy."

I wondered, "How could some kid think we'd only have part of my guinea pig with us?"

Abe looked at Seth. "What does this kid mean?"

"He could have part of the Navy with him, but ALL of it?" Seth looked at Stanley. "Are you lying to us, kid?"

Stanley shook his head. "I'm telling

you the truth. Why would I lie about that? It's nothing to brag about!"

"Is the Navy here on vacation?" Seth asked.

I nodded. "Yes. And if you have a problem with that, you can talk to the campground! They said over the phone that Navy could be here."

Abe spoke really quietly. "They don't look like they're faking it, Seth."

I shook my head. "We sure aren't faking it. If you push Stanley, you might make Navy angry." I could just hear her saying "Burrr-burrr-burrr" if they touched her, and I didn't want her to be worried or upset.

Abe's voice seemed to get quieter and quieter. "U.S. Navy?!"

"Well, American," I corrected. American is Navy's type. It means that she has smooth, straight hair. (Lucky her!)

Had these boys talked to my parents about my guinea pig? They sure seemed interested in her! And scared! I figured maybe they were allergic.

"The one thing wrong," I added, "is

that Navy isn't supposed to be let loose."

Seth's eyes grew even larger, and he nudged Abe with his elbow. "Come on! Let's get out of here!"

Stanley and I looked at each other after the rec center door slammed shut. He reached under his shirt and handed Navy back to me.

"Wow," Stanley said.

"Yeah, wow." I looked at Navy, then back at Stanley. "I don't think they'll be coming back for a long time. Who knew someone could be so scared of a guinea pig? Anyway, let's go. I can't do anything here while holding Navy."

We took Navy back to our campsite. Mom was sitting at the picnic table, and she raised her eyebrows when she saw that Navy was loose.

I put Navy back in the carrier. Stanley even gave her a pat while I was putting her in it. Gave her a pat! I would have jumped up and down right then and there, but I didn't want him to realize he'd done something super duper nice. He might never do it again. I acted calm.

Dad walked up to the campsite before mom could ask any questions. He had a few small fish hanging from a line. "I've got our lunch! What's up? You both look like you've had a fright."

Mom nodded. "I was just thinking the same thing."

I looked at them both. "I don't know how you did it!"

"Did what?" Mom asked.

"I think she means, catching so many fish." Dad smiled a huge smile and pointed at his catch. "I used that new fly. It was amazing! I . . ." He trailed off. "You don't mean the fish, I guess."

"NO." I shook my head. "I mean, I don't know how you scared those two boys about Navy. Navy is just a little guinea pig. What did you say to them?"

Both Mom and Dad looked confused. Mom looked at Dad. "Have you talked to any boys about Navy?"

He shook his head. "The only thing I've been talking to is my fishing pole." He blushed. "He and I are friends."

Mom shook her head, too. "I haven't talked to any boys, myself. I talked to my golf club and asked why it was so lousy. I golfed again and again, and it never got any better! Then, I talked to a couple of squirrels that were sitting on the picnic table, and asked them not to run off with any grapes."

Stanley and I looked at each other. I don't know about him, but I sure was confused.

"What is all this about?" Mom asked.

"Well, we were at the rec center," I said, letting it all out and talking fast. "I was really bad, and I took Navy there without her being in her carrier. And there are these two older boys who are bullies--"

Dad looked down at the fish on his line. "Oh. I did see two boys in the rec center before you made your lanyards. They looked a little bit like they were up to no good."

I scrunched up my nose. "Yes, them."

"In the future," Dad said sternly, "you need to tell your mother and me straightaway if someone isn't treating you properly."

I nodded. "Stanley had Navy hidden under his shirt, because I was scared they would hurt her. They were really worried while we talked about her. I guessed you must have said something about her to scare them, or maybe they're allergic to guinea pigs."

"They kept asking funny questions about her," Stanley added. "Like, if she was from the U.S. and if ALL of Navy was here, or just part of her."

Dad started chuckling. Then Mom joined in.

"What's so funny?" I asked.

Dad finally stopped laughing long enough to talk. "It sounds like they thought you were talking about THE Navy. The military Navy. They thought you were here camping with a branch of the military."

Mom smiled. "No wonder they were worried! I imagine they figured if they picked on you, they would have a whole branch of the military to answer to. I have to say, those boys must have big imaginations, to confuse a guinea pig with the military."

"That's pretty silly," I said. "I'm younger, and I would have never thought that."

"I feel that bullies are some of the most timid people of all if confronted,"

Mom said. "They had a lot to feel guilty over, so it was easy for them to jump to conclusions and worry about getting punished."

Stanley peeked at Navy in her carrier and gave her a thumbs up.

Dad must have gotten tired of holding his catch--although I don't know how since the fish were so tiny--and he hung his fish up on the line stretched between two trees.

"Don't you or Stanley bring me back any more fish," Mom said to him. Her eyebrows pointed down.

"Why not?" He looked hurt. "They won't go to waste."

Mom shook her head. "They won't, but you make ME cook them. Ugh! If any of you go fishing again, it's catch and release from now on."

Dad went into the tent for a minute, and came back out with the camera. "Caroline, take this."

He walked way, way back from the clothesline and put his hand up, as if holding something not really there.

"Walk up close to the fish there, Caroline."

I did.

"Okay," he said. "Now, see if it looks like the fish are really big and I'm really small."

I looked in the viewfinder and laughed. Dad looked like he was holding the line, and beneath it hung fish that were huge. Dad can be really good at taking something bad and sad and scary and quickly helping you find something fun to think about.

I snapped a photo for him, making

sure the clothesline didn't show up in the shot.

"Every camper needs a tall tale fish story," he said as he took the camera back. "Your turn, Stanley!"

That gave me an idea. Later on, we put Navy on the tent floor. I stood in the way back, and had Stanley take a picture. I wanted Navy to be safe in the tent, so I couldn't get far enough away to make her look too big, but it did work a little bit. It looked like this:

That's probably as close as I'll ever get to having a pet capybara.

Thursday

Tonight I'm writing by flashlight because this is the Fourth of July, and we stayed busy all day. The campground let campers set fireworks off at their campsites. There were so many sounds coming from campsites, even during the day. There were all sorts of hisses, pops, and crackles.

I jumped up and down and asked Mom if she had brought along anything for us to use. It's always good to think positively, even if you know your mom likes being cautious and doesn't think fireworks are safe. (At least, maybe, when Stanley is around.) "There are dried pine needles all over the place," she said. "What is this campground thinking?!"

"That they want people to have fun!" I said.

"Well, you wait until it gets dark, and then there's a special surprise I packed," she said.

"Until dark" was a long time to wait, but it's not hard to find things to do when you're camping. Stanley and I went to the rec center, knowing Abe and Seth wouldn't be up to their old tricks.

A lot of kids were there!

"Abe and Seth are just staying at their campsite," Mia said when she saw me. "I've seen them there, and they look nervous or something!"

I told her about what had happened. Stanley told other kids, too, and soon everyone in the rec center talked and laughed about how two bullies had gotten scared by a little guinea pig.

Mia and I played table tennis, while Stanley and Max--the boy who had helped Stanley ignore the lanyard craft--used the shuffleboard table. It felt nice being able to use the rec center and not worrying about anyone coming in to kick us out. We stayed for a long time before heading back to the campsite.

When it got dark out, Mom showed us her surprise. She had brought along some clear plastic sticks with liquid in them. They glow when you bend and shake them. She had strung them on string so we could wear them. Stanley and I each bent a stick, put the strings around our necks, and waved the sticks around.

Firework for kids with worrywart moms.

Well, at least I ended up with some sort of a lanyard. Stanley took my REAL one apart, because he wanted the gimp for shoelaces.

Stanley and I saw lights in the campsite next to ours. We walked to the edge of our campsite to watch. A few kids ran around with sparklers. They swayed the lights around, and drew with them in the air. As the sparklers burned bright, I could make out what types of things they spelled and drew--things like curlicues, letters, and circles. Just like magic!

Stanley ran over to ask them for a couple. He can be very brave, but maybe not so polite.

He came back with two. Mom looked upset.

"Aw, it's the Fourth. Come on." Dad sounded like a little kid with how he begged for her to give in.

Mom sighed. "Oh, all right. But, you two have to hold the sparklers by the tippy tip tips, and no running around. And no moving the sparklers around the way those kids are doing. You are to stay still as can be. I don't want those hot sparks landing on any of these pine needles."

I guess dangerous things aren't much fun, after all.

Something like that can zap the fun out of doing something dangerous, but I guess moms have to step in sometimes to be careful. Especially since we're only borrowing Stanley.

Mom and Dad always tell me it's good to return borrowed things in like-new condition.

Friday

We left the campground this morning. I watched as Mom and Dad packed up all of the supplies. There went the outdoor kitchen, there went our home-away-from-home (also known as a tent with the scent of the garage), there went the nice pine smell of being outdoors in the woods. Stanley and I rolled up our sleeping bags and made sure we had everything packed away in our suitcases. I had to sit on mine even harder this time, because I'd found some neat-looking pinecones.

I felt a little bit sad, but it's also nice to go back home, where everything you are familiar with is. Like your best friend. Your room. Not to mention, the nearest bathroom isn't half a mile away.

I'm sure Navy was thinking, "All right!

I get to go back to my big cage!" Being cooped up in her tub and carrier probably hasn't been as fun for her as it has been for me to have her along.

I'm going to have more room-- yay!

As we drove out of the campground, we passed other people's campsites. I saw Abe and Seth. They sat at a picnic table, bouncing a ball off it.

"There are those kids who acted like they owned the rec center," I said to Mom and Dad.

"I suppose we ought to tell them the truth," Mom said. "You didn't mean to, but it's not entirely honest to let them believe that the entire Navy is here on a camping trip."

Stanley yelled out the car window: "You want to see the Navy?"

I thought it was a little rotten of him, adding the "the." Adding it made it sound even more like MY Navy was the one they were worried about.

They scrambled to get up, and ran away into their tent.

Stanley and I laughed. It felt kind of good seeing them get scared again, after how mean they'd been.

"Kids," Mom said. She used that type of voice where, even though she wasn't bawling us out or saying much, you could tell she was bawling us out just the same.

"We'd better get out." Dad turned the car off.

"Aw, Dad!" I complained. I knew it wouldn't be right to tell a fib to people, even if we hadn't MEANT to. But it didn't feel too fun knowing we had to talk to them about it.

Stanley, Dad, and I got out of the car. Mom stayed with Navy.

"Stanley and Caroline have something to tell you," Dad said to the tent. Normally, he maybe wouldn't talk to a tent, but you kind of have to when there are people inside it and there's no way to knock on the door.

We heard a Z-I-I-I-P sound, and out popped Seth's head. "Wh-what is it?" He sounded scared. Really scared.

He looked like a turtle!

"The Navy isn't here," I said. "Just A Navy, but not THE Navy."

"Go on, Caroline," Dad prompted me.

Both Abe and Seth came out of the tent.

"Navy is the name of my guinea pig. Navy Red." I felt my face go all hot and uncomfortable. But then I looked at Abe and Seth. THEIR faces were red, too. The whole thing probably made them feel pretty silly about themselves.

I still think navy red could be a color.

Neither one of them said anything. They just kept looking at us with their red faces.

I didn't know what to say next. Mom would probably have wanted me to apologize, but I hadn't done anything wrong to them. We hadn't known what they had thought about Navy. I didn't know what to say, so I finally blurted out: "Oh, and Stanley hit Abe with a paddle."

Dad looked at Stanley. "Stanley, you need to apologize for THAT."

Stanley scowled at Abe. "I'm sorry you made me wallop you with a paddle."

Dad looked a little upset, but then he just shrugged. I guess you're not allowed to get too cross with a kid you're only borrowing.

Dad motioned for us to get back into the car.

On the way home, I thought about how we had had a really fun time camping. I realized maybe Stanley, Navy, and I could be good friends after all. Stanley hadn't really annoyed me during the camping trip! Well, I don't think he had tried to, anyway. Maybe nothing bad would ever come between us again!

Just as I was thinking this, Stanley shifted a bit so that he could see me. He placed his gimp-laced shoes on the center bump of the car floor.

"By the way, that Friday we left?" Stanley picked at his knee scab.

I raised my eyebrows. "Yeah?"

He looked up at me again. "You had a postcard out in the kitchen."

I nodded. "And?" I figured he'd tell me how funny I had been with answering all the questions as if Navy had.

"I did something nice for you."

"What was that, Stanley?"

He smiled. "I put it out in your mailbox!"

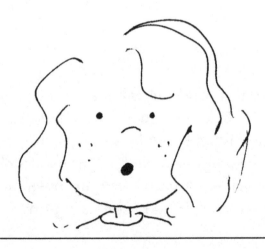

About the author and illustrator

Melissa J. Taylor got Violet, her first guinea pig, when she was nine years old. She even wrote and illustrated books about her, just like Caroline! The illustrations in the Caroline's Cavy series are inspired by Melissa's drawings from her childhood, such as these two drawings of Violet and self-portrait.

Melissa is also the author of the Guinea Pigs' Storybook series, which follows eight guinea pig friends through a year of adventures.

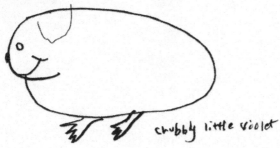

chubby little violet

Made in the USA
Las Vegas, NV
04 September 2021